I Am the Desert

Anthony D. Fredericks

Illustrations by Jesse Reisch

Rio
Chico
BOOKS FOR CHILDREN

Anthony D. Fredericks is the author of over 125 books, including more than three dozen award-winning children's books, such as *Desert Night Desert Day* and *Around One Cactus*. He attended high school and college in Arizona and now lives in South-Central Pennsylvania. He is a professor of education at York College.

Encouraged by her parents, Jesse Reisch started drawing at the age of two. After attending art schools in Chicago, she lived in Asia and Europe, where her artistic sensibilities blossomed. Jesse's artwork can be found in countless books and magazines. Today she lives in San Miguel de Allende, Mexico, surrounded by the colors you see in this book.

Rio Chico, an imprint of Rio Nuevo Publishers®
P. O. Box 5250
Tucson, AZ 85703-0250
(520) 623-9558, www.rionuevo.com

Text © 2017 by Anthony D. Fredericks
Illustrations © 2017 by Jesse Reisch

First Paperback Edition, 2017
ISBN: 978-1-940322-28-5

Editorial: Theresa Howell
Book design: David Jenney

Printed in China.

5   4   3   19   20   21

The Library of Congress has cataloged the hardcover edition as follows:

Library of Congress Cataloging-in-Publication Data

Fredericks, Anthony D.
 I am the desert / by Anthony D. Fredericks ;
illustrated by Jesse Reisch.
    p. cm.
Summary: The living desert tells about its quiet beauty, the plants and animals that it sustains, people who have sought water in its vast expanse, and how it continues to change. Includes facts about the Sonoran Desert.
 ISBN 978-1-933855-73-8 (alk. paper)
 [1. Deserts—Fiction. 2. Sonoran Desert—Fiction.] I. Reisch, Jesse, ill. II. Title.
 PZ7.F872292Iah 2012
 [E]—dc23
                            2012006015

For the loves of my life: Phyllis, Rebecca, and Jonathan
—A.D.F.

To Bodin for his courageous spirit and gentle friendship
—J.R.

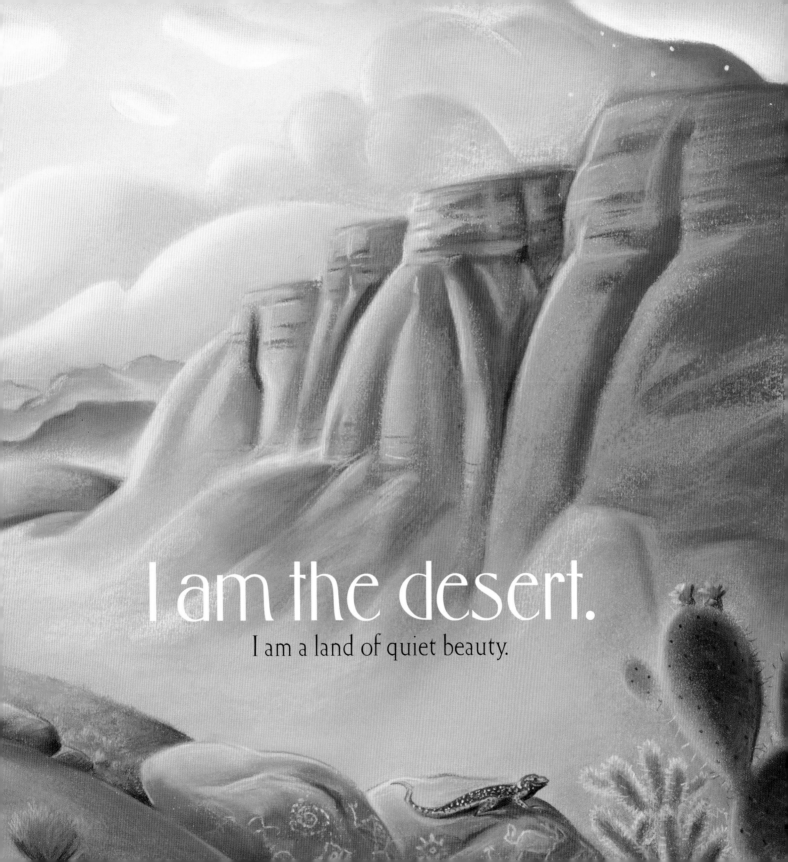

I am the desert.

I am a land of quiet beauty.

I am sandy hills, tall mesas,
and wind-washed boulders.
I am thousands of miles
and hundreds of tales.

I am rich with strong survivors.

I am alive.

I am the scuttle of
sharp-tailed scorpions dancing in circles.
I am the leap of kangaroo rats
hopping across cool sand.
I am the whir of bats
venturing out to cover the night.

I am a sea of cactus plants.
Come closer and you will see tiny babies
just born, resting quietly
in deep saguaro holes.

I am the roadrunner
flashing across my pebbled surface.
I am the coiled serpent
hidden beneath a creosote bush.
So too am I the beaded Gila monster
hiding under rocks...and the blooming cereus
opening its flowers in the dark.

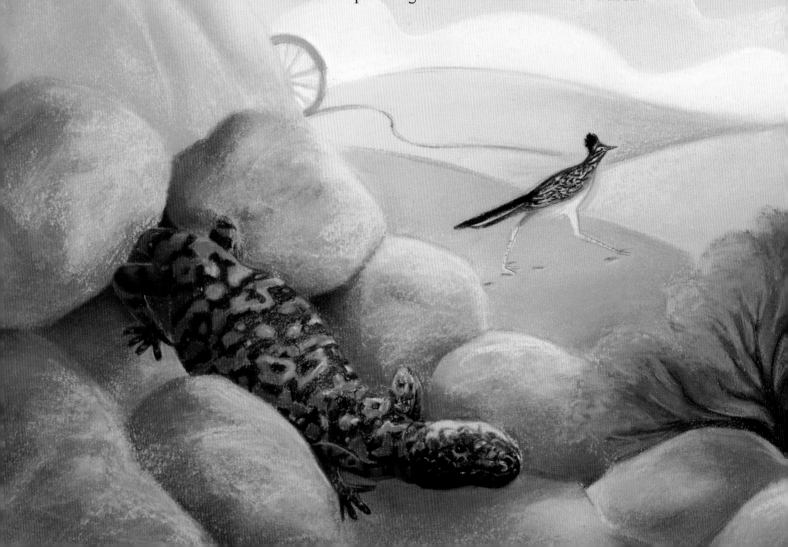

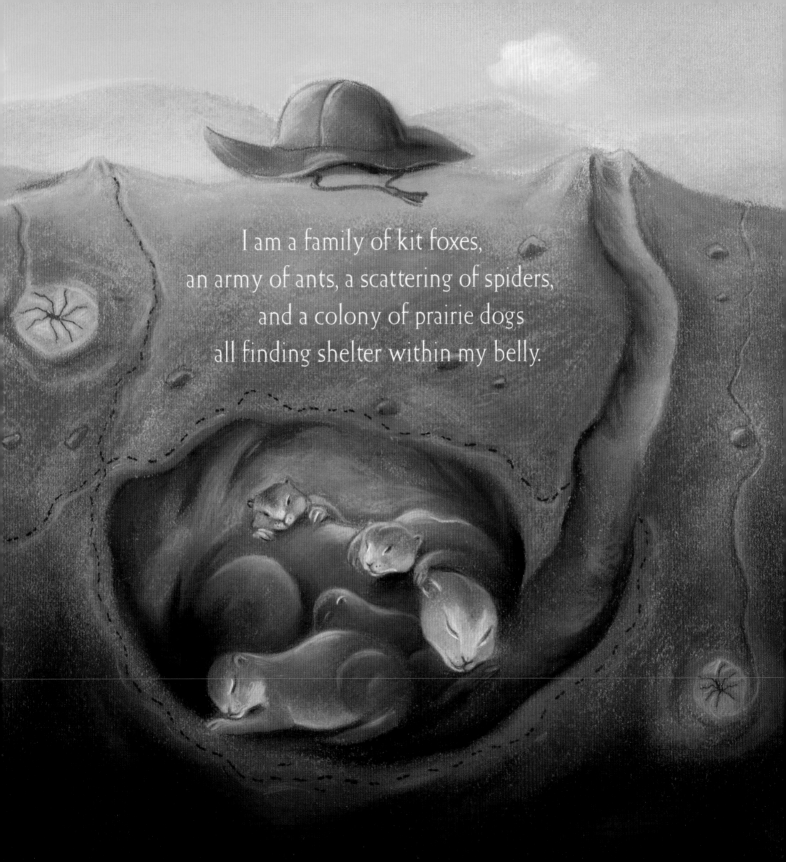

I am a family of kit foxes,
an army of ants, a scattering of spiders,
and a colony of prairie dogs
all finding shelter within my belly.

I am timeless.

I have been here for millions of years
and will be here for millions more.
But I am never the same.
I am ever evolving.
Strong winds blast sand against my rocks.
Spires and time-worn arches
are sculpted from my face.
My canyons and deep arroyos
are shaped slowly and forever.

Sudden rains stir spadefoot toads
beneath my surface.
They crawl upward, find a mate, and lay eggs.
They leave behind knots of tadpoles
who must quickly grow into adults.
Before the puddles dry, they too slip underground;
once more to wait...wait...wait.

Brief showers
bring glorious wildflowers.
Carpets of orange and purple and yellow
lie across my back.
Bright colors sweep across the earth
and up to the horizon.

The sun, hot and bright, looms overhead.

It is a constant reminder of who I am.

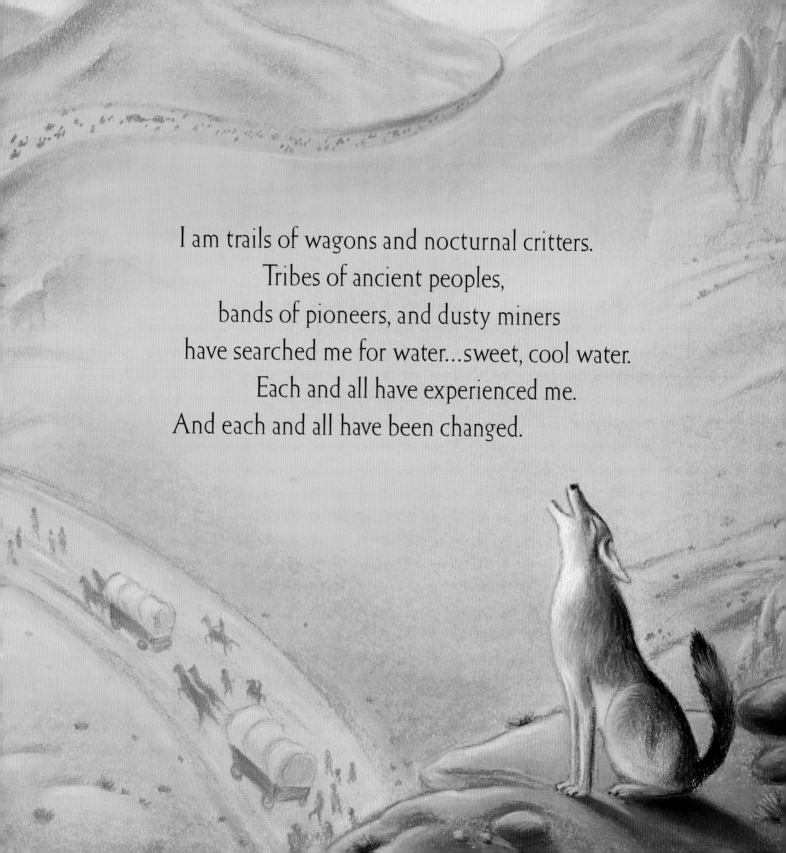

I am trails of wagons and nocturnal critters.
Tribes of ancient peoples,
bands of pioneers, and dusty miners
have searched me for water...sweet, cool water.
Each and all have experienced me.
And each and all have been changed.

I, too, continue to change.
Clouds shuffle over me,
drawing shadows and lines across my features.
Dunes rise up and fall again.
The wind embraces me, and slowly—
ever so slowly—changes my form.
I am forever new again.

I am a land of discovery.
For here, there is much to learn.
Come and look.
I will share with you my rock-ribbed valleys,
my crimson cliffs,
and my layered miles of spine-studded plants
and brilliant creatures.
Come find my beauty!

I am the desert.

I am the Sonoran Desert.

I am 120,000 square miles big. I extend across southern Arizona, southeastern California, and the northwest Mexican states of Sonora (for whom I am named), Baja California, and Baja California Sur. In fact, one-half of me is in Mexico. My immediate relatives include the Mojave Desert in California, the Great Basin Desert in Nevada and Utah, and the Chihuahuan Desert in Mexico.

Many parts of me get less than three inches of rain each year.

That's not very much rain! During the day my temperature may soar above 100 degrees. In winter I may drop to a temperature of around 32 degrees. Often, my temperatures differ by more than 50 degrees between noon and midnight.

My largest relative is the Sahara Desert

in northern Africa. It is larger than the entire United States (more than 3,500,000 square miles). It has also recorded the highest temperature in the world: 136° F (58° C).

I have more than 2,000 native species of plants.

I also have more than 100 reptile species,
20 amphibian species, 30 fish species,
350 bird species, and 60 mammal species.

I am filled with life!

I am the only place
in the world where the famous saguaro
cactus grows in the wild.

You might not think so, but I am in danger.
People drive across me, leave their garbage
behind, and sometimes harm the plants or
take the animals that are part of me.

Please be careful
when you visit!

Visit me often

Leave only...